inventions

and some real ones too.

By Roger McGough

illustrated by Holly Swain

NAME : PROFESSOR
DOTTY
DABBLE
AGE : 25 YEARS
BORN : LINCOLN
JOB : INVENTOR

NAME : DIGBY
AGE : 43 LIGHT
YEARS
BORN : OUT THERE
JOB : LABORATORY
ASSISTANT

FRANCES LINCOLN CHILDREN'S BOOKS

"**D**oor, Digby, door," called out Professor Dotty Dabble, up to her elbows in a spaghetti of electrical wiring.

Digby scuttled up the wall and across the ceiling to collect the morning mail.

Telephone Bill

Prof-D-Dabble

Without bothering to open the envelopes, Digby x-rayed their contents:

"Telephone bill... gas bill... water bill... duck bill... *Mad Inventor's Monthly*, and an invitation to enter your best invention and win the holiday of a lifetime."

"Where?" asked Dotty.

"At the National Science Museum."

"Humph! Doesn't sound like
the holiday of a lifetime to me."

"No, that's not the prize," said Digby,
"that's where the competition
is taking place."

"Oh, in that case, Digby, I think
we should enter. The only trouble is,
which invention do we choose?"

Digby listed some of Dotty's most famous gadgets:

A chocolate cup — Simply add hot water and drink before it melts.

A mobile phone booth for shy mobile phone users.

The Mower-glider — hang glide and mow the lawn at the same time.

Voice-activated socks.

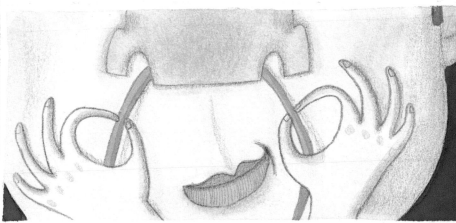

Nasal-floss—the last word in nasal hygiene.

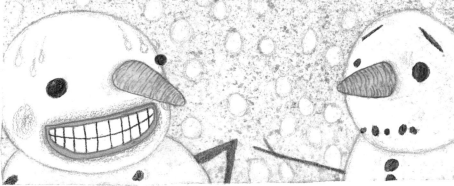

Centrally-heated birdcages—for budgies who like to be outside in winter.

Thermal dentures—false teeth that keep the mouth warm.

When he had finished, Digby looked at the pen in his hand.

"Is this one of your inventions too, Professor?" he asked.

"Probably," said Dotty in a mumbly sort of voice.

Digby's mouse clicked on to BALLPOINT to see if the professor was correct.

Ladislo Biro invented the first
ball-point pen in 1938.
Biro was a Hungarian journalist
who wanted to write with an ink
that dried quickly and didn't smudge.

AHHHH!

Unfortunately, the newspaper ink that was most suitable
was too thick to be used with a pen-nib,

feather

twig

drinking
straw

plastic
tubing

plastic
tubing
and a pea!

so he made a pen with a tiny ball in its tip...

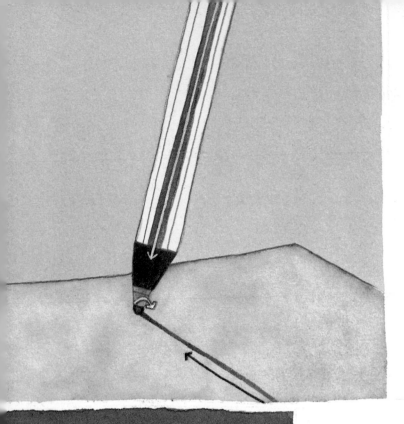

As the pen moves along,
the ball rotates, picking up
ink from the cartridge
and leaving it on the paper.

If Ladislo's surname had been Wifflepoof,
would we be using wifflepoof pens?

Digby and Dotty packed all the inventions into the Gizmobile, and set off for the National Science Museum.

"I wish the rain would stop," yelled Dotty above the rattle-tattle of the engine. "I can hardly see where I'm going."

"Then why not switch on the wipers?" suggested Digby.

"Good idea," said Dotty. But it didn't help.

"Wouldn't they work better if they were on the outside of the car?" asked Digby.

Dotty thought for a moment.

"Mmmmm," she said, "perhaps that's why my invention isn't working."

Digby wondered who really invented the wiper and clicked his mouse.

DIGBY. W. WIPERS.

Known as windscreen wipers in Britain, they are called windshield wipers in America, where they were invented by Mary Anderson in 1903. She saw that tram drivers had to open the windows of their cars when it rained in order to see where they were driving.

So she invented a wiper that would clean rain, sleet or snow from the windshield by using a handle inside the car.

By 1916 all US cars were sold with wipers.

"I think I'll fly above the rain clouds," said Dotty.
"Hold on to your nuts and bolts, Digby. Here we go!"
   The Gizmobile sprouted a pair of wings
and took to the air. Soon they were flying
in the clear blue sky, high above the clouds.

"Better put one of these on just in case," said Dotty
cheerfully, handing Digby a parachute.
"Is this one of your inventions too?" asked Digby.
"More or less," replied Dotty in a muttery sort of voice.
Digby clicked on to PARACHUTE to check it out.

DIGBY·PARACHUTE·

A Frenchman called Louis-Sebastien Lenormand could claim to be the first parachutist when, in 1783, he bravely jumped from a tall tree holding an umbrella in each hand, and drifted to the ground.

Two years later, encouraged by his success, he went up in a hot-air balloon to test his home-made parachute. But not on himself.

He attached the parachute to a small basket containing his pet dog and dropped it over the side.

Happily for everybody, especially the dog, it landed safely.

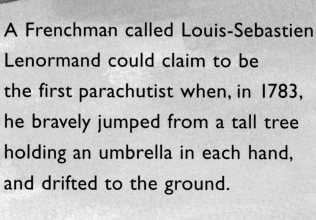

The first person to jump from a plane
and survive was Lieutenant Harold R Harris.
He parachuted out of his plane during
a training mission in 1922 and landed
in a vineyard.

"I'm feeling peckish," said Dotty. "Let's find the nearest cafe."

As they flew lower, Digby suddenly spotted a UFO spinning alongside the Gizmobile.

"Look Professor, a flying saucer!"

Dotty laughed. "That's not a flying saucer! That's a Frisbee."

"Of course," said Digby feeling a little silly, "another of your inventions, was it?"

SLOW

DIGBY. FRISBEE.

But the professor was concentrating hard on landing
the Gizmobile, so Digby clicked his mouse on to FRISBEE.

The Frisbee Baking Company of Bridgeport, Connecticut in the USA sold pies to hungry college students.

The students found out that the empty pie tins could be tossed and caught, so a new game was invented.

In 1948, Walter Frederick Morrison invented
a plastic version that could fly further
and with greater accuracy than the tin plate.

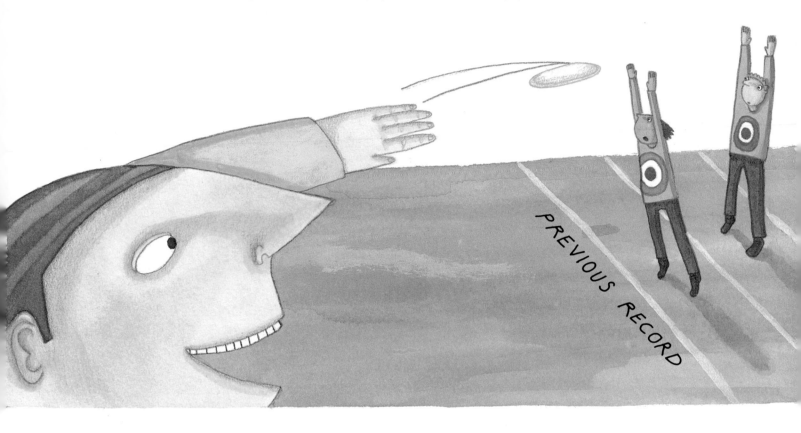

PREVIOUS RECORD

By 1955 his improved *Pluto Platter* coincided with the growing
interest in UFOs and flying saucers. This made him a millionaire.

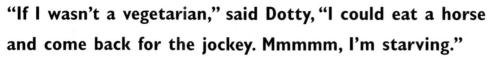

"If I wasn't a vegetarian," said Dotty, "I could eat a horse
and come back for the jockey. Mmmmm, I'm starving."
   She piled her plate high but in a hurry to pay the cashier,
she tripped over one of her laces. Cheese, lettuce, tomatoes,
carrots, apple pie and custard went flying through
the air like a scrumptious rainbow.

Digby asked why the professor didn't wear shoes
that fastened with velcro.

"Good idea," said Dotty cheerfully.

"Trust me not to use one of my best inventions."

DIGBY. VELCRO.

CLOSE UP

Digby had his doubts about this so while
Dotty tucked in, he clicked on to VELCRO.

George de Mestral, a Swiss inventor and keen mountaineer, got the idea for velcro after he had taken his dog for a walk in the countryside.

When the dog came home its coat was covered with burrs, which are those little plant seed-sacs that cling to fabric (and hairy dogs).

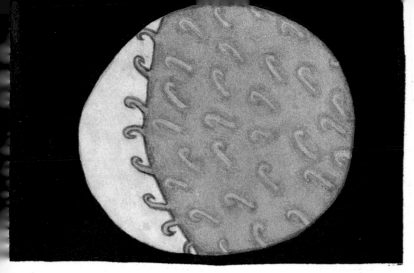

George de Mestral looked at the burrs under his microscope and saw that they had tiny hooks which latch on to soft material.

He then set about making a fastener for clothing which used the same idea. He called it velcro, a combination of the words *velour* and *crochet*.

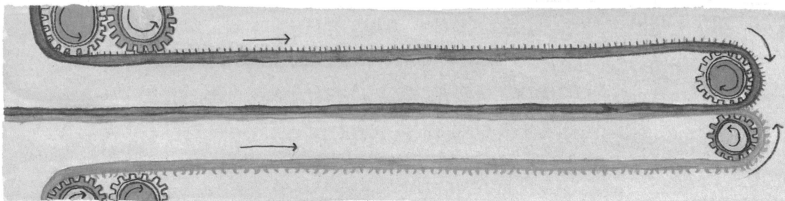

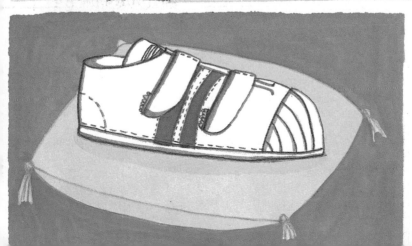

At first everyone laughed at his invention, but now millions of yards of velcro are sold every year.

The National Science Museum was choc-a-block. People had travelled from all over the world to marvel, puzzle and applaud the weird and wonderful inventions on display. There were...

Pens that corrected your spelling as you wrote.

Tables that could lay themselves.

Umbrellas with built-in stereos.

Welcome Back!

49

Walking sticks that could find their own way home.

nearly there Digby !

science museum

Digital deckchairs that would fold and unfold at the touch of a button.

HA HAHA

Stringless yo-yos

Edible school scarves for those boring long queues at bus stops.

"Oh dear," said Dotty, "I'm never going to win with my soppy collection of useless inventions."

"Never mind," said Digby. "It's not the winning that's important, but the oodle, ardle, oodle."

"If you say so," said the professor.

Just then, the judges called for silence.

"Ladies and gentlemen, the winner of the competition for the best invention is..."

"Well, who'd have thought," said Dotty, enjoying her first giant banana split of the holiday, "that I would win first prize for inventing you?"

"Congratulations," said Digby.

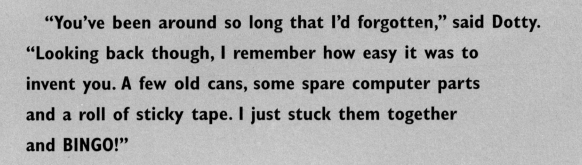

"You've been around so long that I'd forgotten," said Dotty. "Looking back though, I remember how easy it was to invent you. A few old cans, some spare computer parts and a roll of sticky tape. I just stuck them together and BINGO!"

Digby didn't say anything. He just smiled and clicked on DIGBY...

DIGBY.ME.